MARVIN'S FUNNY DANCE

Meerkats come from Africa. They live in burrows under the ground and have big families of 20 or 30. Can you imagine sharing your house with that many brothers and sisters?

For my fantastic Mum and Dad

First published in 2008
by Hodder Children's Books

Text and illustrations copyright © Sarah McConnell 2008

Hodder Children's Books
338 Euston Road
London NW1 3BH

Hodder Children's Books Australia
Level 17/207 Kent Street
Sydney, NSW 2000

A catalogue record of this book is available from the British Library.

ISBN: 978 0 340 93188 2
002

Printed in China

Hodder Children's Books is a division of Hachette Children's Books
An Hachette Livre UK Company
www.hachettelivre.co.uk

MARVIN'S FUNNY DANCE

Sarah McConnell

Hodder
Children's
Books

A division of Hachette Children's Books

Early one morning, Marvin Meerkat squeezed himself out of his cold dark burrow and into the hot African sun. Moe was already up as usual doing the stretching exercises for meercadets.

'Morning Marve,' said Moe chirpily.

'Huumph,' grumbled Marvin. 'Have I missed anything?'

'Nope,' said Moe. 'Same as usual.'

Marvin was in a grumpy mood – he hated morning meercadets:
every day it was the same old thing.

You see Marvin liked to be different. He gave Moe a little wink...

...and began wiggling his hips,

waggling his toes,

rubbing his tummy

and touching his nose.

'Marvin Meer!'

shouted Thelma the Chief
meerkat at the top of her voice.

'Stop that *now* and
be serious for once.'

But Marvin couldn't be serious, no matter how hard he tried. His head was too full of cheeky tricks and crazy ideas.

'I just like making people laugh,' he told Moe. But, most of the time, no one laughed, except for Moe of course.

'That Marvin is such a show off,' they said.

One morning, two big brown birds called the Buzzard Brothers were spotted in the distance.

The Buzzard Brothers were bully birds and they were always bothering the meerkat family.

But it was so hot that day that nearly all the meerkats had drifted into a deep sleep.

Even wide-awake Warren
had dropped off and
he was supposed to be
the lookout.

Only Marvin was still awake, with no one
to play with and nothing to do.
Suddenly a mischievous idea popped into his head.

'He, he, he! This will make them
laugh,' he chuckled.

He cupped his
paws around his
mouth and...

'SQUAWK! SQUAWK!'

went Marvin, exactly like
a bad-tempered buzzard.

The meerkats went wild, leaping here, leaping there and diving into their burrows.

Old Bertie was shaking like a leaf and cousin Clarence fell out of his tree. Even Moe got a fright.

'Uh oh,' said Marvin when he saw what he had done. 'Now I'm in trouble.'

'Marvin,' said Thelma. 'You've gone too far!'
And she sent him to his burrow to think
about what he had done.

'Sorry,' said Marvin sadly.
'I just thought it would be fun.'

Outside Moe shook his head. Marvin had made him think. 'The Buzzard Brothers have bullied us for too long,' he said.

'But I've got a plan. We need a tree, some dung balls and plenty of guts,' and he rushed off to tell the others.

The meerkats worked fast.
They pulled and they puffed, they
heaved and they huffed until there it was
– a spectacular bird-scaring contraption.

Then, all of a sudden, wide-awake
Warren chirped the alarm call.

The Buzzard Brothers
were back!

But the meerkats weren't
ready and they lost their nerve.

They're not the bravest
of animals, you know.

'What are we going to do?' said Warren,
when the birds had gone.
'Hmmm,' said cousin Clarence. 'We need someone to
distract the brothers so our plan will work. But who?'

'It has to be someone brave,'
said Moe, smiling. 'Someone who doesn't
mind standing out from the crowd...
a bit of a show off maybe.'

`Marvin!'
they all said at once!

Moe went to find him.
'Marve,' he said.
'We need your help!'
And quickly he whispered
the plan in Marvin's ear.

Marvin gave a little wink and crept up the hill, which overlooked the meerkats' burrow.

When he reached the top, he began to dance just like he had that morning.

He twirled,
he moved,
he swirled,
he grooved,

like no other meerkat had ever danced before.

The birds spotted him
and started flapping towards him,
but this time the meerkats were ready...

The birds swerved as the dung balls shot through the air. They went right, they went left, but it was too much for them.

'We've never had to put up with this before,' the Buzzard Brothers complained.

And in a flurry of feathers, they were gone:
two little dots in the distance – and they
never came back.

How the meerkats whooped and cheered.

Marvin ran down the hill to join the others and when he got to the bottom, do you know what he saw?